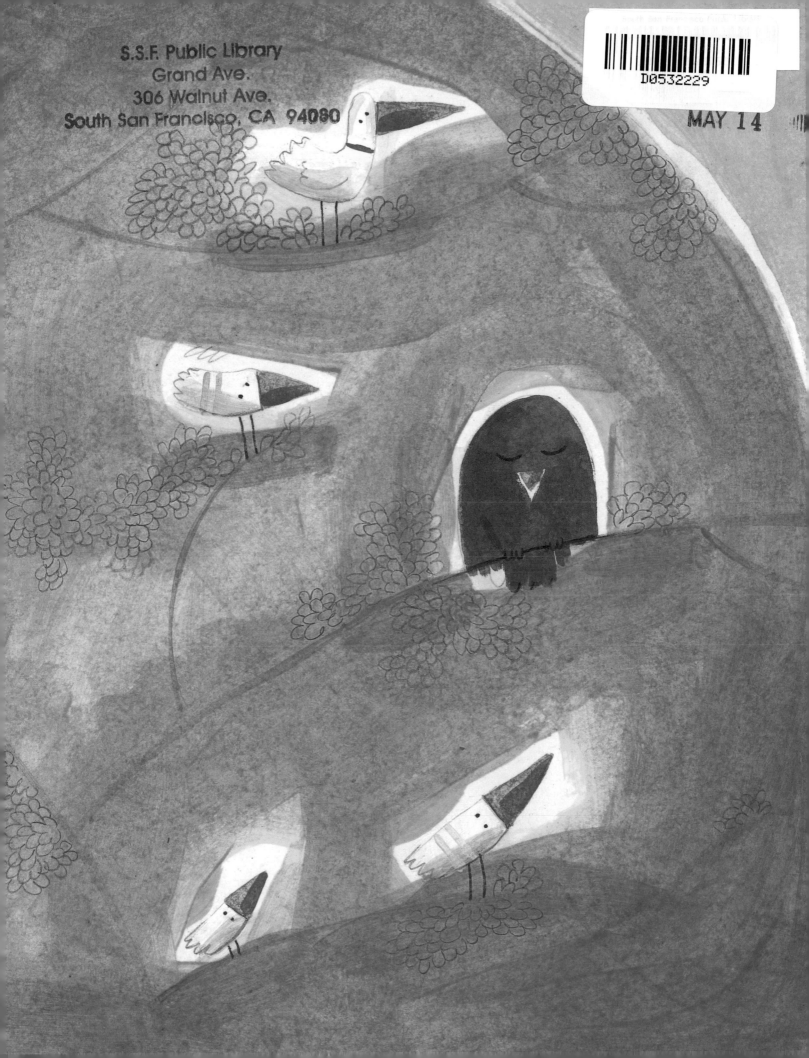

Text copyright © 2013
by Harriet Ziefert
Illustrations copyright © 2013
by Barroux

Use of lyrics permission:
"I Said Good Morning"
by Betty Comden, Adolph Green,
and Andre G. Previn © 1959
(renewed) Stratford Music
Corporation (ASCAP)
All rights administered by
Chappell & Co., Inc.

CIP data is available.
Published in the United States by
 Blue Apple Books
515 Valley Street
Maplewood, NJ 07040
www.blueapplebooks.com
First edition 07/13
Printed in China
ISBN: 978-1-60905-374-1

10 9 8 7 6 5 4 3 2 1

HARRIET
ZIEFERT

IT'S TIME to SAY
GOOD NIGHT

illustrations by

BARROUX

BLUE APPLE

to the sun,

Good Morning
to the hills,

Good Morning

to the chickies and the hen.

Good Morning

to the rooster,

Good Morning
to the cow,

Good Morning
to the piggies in the pen.

Good Morning
to the grass,

Good
Morning
to the trees,

Good Morning

to the birdies

and the bees.

Good Morning
to the garden,

Good Morning
to the earth,

Good Morning
to the water and the seeds.

Good Morning to the planes,

Good Morning to the buses,

Good Morning to the taxis and the vans.

Good Morning to the garbage and the cans.

Good Morning! Good Morning!

To everything in sight!

By the time
I get through saying

Good Morning,

it's time to say . . .

Good Night to the trucks,

Good Night to the cars,

Good Night to the garbage and the cans.

Good Night to the planes,

Good Night to the buses,

Good Night to the taxis and the vans.

Good Night to the grass,
Good Night to the trees,

Good Night to the birdies and the bees.

Good Night to the garden,

Good Night to the earth,

Good Night to the water and the seeds.

Good Night

to the rooster,

Good Night
to the cow,

Good Night to the piggies in the pen.

Good Night

to the sun,

Good Night
to the hills,

Good Night
to the chickies and the hen.

Good night,
good night,

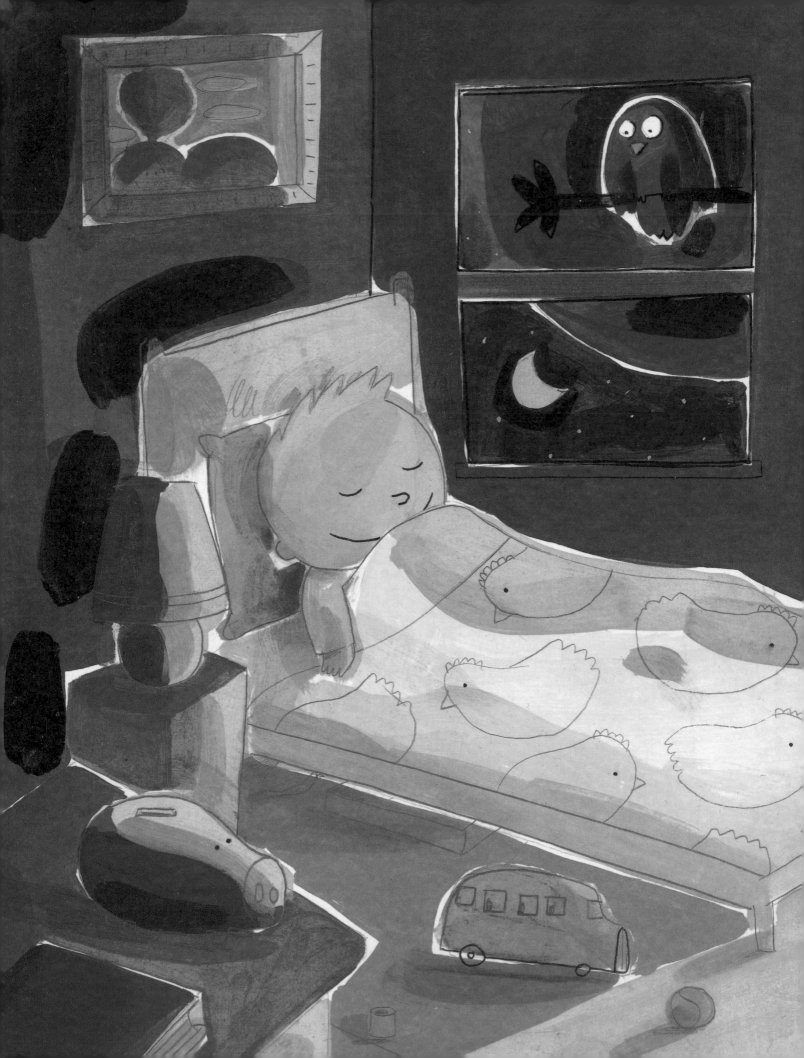

It's time to get

some sleep.

Good Night!